WE WON, WE WON!!

"It wasn't a dream," said Daisy, "and we didn't make it up."

"You really won!" said Delphie. "All you have to do is take the ticket in to Tommy Tucker's and collect the money."

"Well, I can settle this easily, once and for all," said Mr. Green, picking up the telephone and dialing a number.

"Hello, Tommy Tucker's? Could you tell me what the winning lottery number is, please?" Mr. Green listened to the reply. "Thank you very much," he said. He hung up the phone. "Now," he said. "The winning number is 45707."

He walked over to Delphie and took the ticket from his hand. He read it out loud. "See, this ticket says 45707."

Mrs. Green went over and looked at the ticket herself. Then she sat down. Her face was white.

Daisy couldn't tell if her parents were upset about all the money, or pleased.

Weekly Reader Book Club Presents

LOTTERY LUCK

WINNING TICKET!

Judy Delton

Illustrated by S. D. Schindler

Hyperion Books for Children
New York

This book is a presentation of Newfield Publications, Inc.
Newfield Publications offers book clubs for children from
preschool through high school. For further information
write to: **Newfield Publications, Inc.,**
4343 Equity Drive, Columbus, Ohio 43228.

Published by arrangement with Hyperion Books for Children.
Newfield Publications is a federally registered
trademark of Newfield Publications, Inc.
Weekly Reader is a federally registered trademark
of Weekly Reader Corporation.

1995 edition

Library of Congress Cataloging-in-Publication Data
Delton, Judy.
Winning ticket! / Judy Delton; illustrated by S. D. Schindler.–1st ed.
p. cm.–(Lottery luck; #1)
Summary: At the suggestion of her friend Lois, ten-year-old Daisy Green
and her younger brother convince their aunt to buy a lottery ticket that
turns the Green family into millionaires.
ISBN 0-7868-1018-1
[1. Lotteries–Fiction. 2. Family life–Fiction.]
I. Schindler, S. D., ill.
II. Title. III. Series: Delton, Judy. Lottery luck; #1.
PZ7.D388Wi 1995
[Fic]–dc20 94-37188

For Elizabeth Hollow,
who, for one brief shining year,
brought back the old Max Perkins's days of editing.
Thanks for not only *laughing* at the Greens' escapades,
but also for enhancing and enlarging the stories,
and getting the series off to a good start.

—J. D.

LOTTERY LUCK

WINNING TICKET!

CHAPTER 1

"Bring that dirt inside, dear," said Daisy's mother.

Most mothers said *don't* bring that dirt inside, thought Daisy. No matter how much she tried to think of her family as normal, they weren't. Her friends' mothers worked in offices or stayed home and kept house. Daisy's mother played in dirt. She grew flowers on the roof of their condo building.

Her friends' fathers were dentists or garbage collectors. Daisy's father made copper alligators for people's lawns. They came in three pieces and looked like they were partly underwater, ready to spring up and eat you at any minute. Mr. Green also mended copper roofs.

"That's fine black soil!" Mrs. Green went on. "My ivy cuttings will love it!"

Daisy's best friend Lois carried the pail of dirt up the steps. And then up more steps, past the third-floor condo where Daisy lived with her parents and her brother, Delphie. And then up steeper steps through a hole in the ceiling to the roof. The condo building had no yard. Lois lived two blocks away in a real house with a real yard and lots of real dirt. So she snuck a pail or two to the Greens when she came over.

Mrs. Green looked furtively around the corner for the caretaker, Mr. Wong. He owned one of the condos and was president of the condo association. He had given Mrs. Green permission to have a garden on the roof, but he had added, "Not too much weight up there, Iris. We don't want those posies falling down through your ceiling, now do we?"

"Dirt is heavy," said Lois, puffing as she made her way up the last two steps.

"That's just what Mr. Wong says," said Daisy.

Lois set the pail of dirt on the roof and the two girls went back down to Daisy's condo. They walked around two copper mountain goats and a stone reindeer, and washed their hands in the bathroom. Then they went into Daisy's room. On the way they sidestepped rakes and hoes and seed catalogs. They squeezed past a zebra that still needed stripes.

"You guys could use a bigger house," said Lois.

"We're going to get a real house as soon as my dad sells a few more alligators," said Daisy. "The alligators bring in the most money."

Both girls were thinking the same thing. When would he sell another alligator? In Liberty, the small Minnesota town where they lived, there was very little demand for copper three-piece alligators. Or mountain goats or zebras or reindeer. There weren't even many copper roofs to be mended.

"He's got some alligators on display in Minneapolis," said Daisy. "In garden shops and stuff."

"Maybe your mom should go to work, meanwhile," said Lois.

"She does work," said Daisy. "She's a landscape artist."

"I know," said Lois. "But I mean a real job with a paycheck."

Daisy agreed with Lois, but she knew there was no reasoning with adults. She and Delphie often left the newspaper open to the want ads, but their father cut it up for the birdcage, and their mother flipped it over to the sports section. They didn't take the free help they were given. They were hopeless.

"I know one thing," said Daisy. "When I grow up I'm going to be a doctor or a mail carrier. Something with a future. And a regular paycheck."

Daisy liked things to be dependable. Friends, jobs, allowances, meals, the seasons. And parents.

Especially parents. She hated uncertainty. She hated change. She liked her clothes in neat piles in her drawers and her combs and brushes lined up on her dressing table.

"What are we going to do today?" asked Lois. "Should we go to a movie?"

"I have no money," said Daisy.

"How about the library?" asked Lois.

"I've read all the books," said Daisy.

"I have too." Lois sighed. There weren't too many books in their small library. The librarian, Miss Nelson, called them on the phone if a new book came in.

"Summer is boring," said Daisy. "And it's only June."

"Maybe we should find you a job," said Lois. "I mean, then you'd have movie money. And you could help pay for a new house in case those alligators don't sell."

"It's illegal," said Daisy. "You can't get a job when you're ten."

"I mean the kind of job where no one knows you're working," said Lois. "Like baby-sitting or raking or running errands or delivering phone books."

Daisy perked up. Maybe it was time to take the family's future into her own small hands. Her father's statues were working their way into her bedroom. And that roof garden wasn't getting any lighter. Her mother was considering a crop of field corn in the spring.

"What would be even better," said Lois, "would be to win some money. That would be faster. My uncle's mother-in-law won two hundred dollars in the lottery last month. She bought a VCR."

"Two hundred dollars!" whistled Daisy. "It would take us a long time to earn two hundred dollars baby-sitting!"

"Not 'us,'" said Lois. "You. My allowance is enough for me. Although I guess I could use more money if I won it."

"A dream for a dollar," Daisy said. "That's what they say on TV. We've got the dream! All we need is the dollar! Then we could go to movies every day. And even get out of this small place."

Daisy looked around her room. Actually she loved it. It was nice and neat and there were twin beds side by side with matching spreads. The extra one was for Daisy's grandma when she came, or Lois when she stayed over. Suddenly Daisy felt ashamed of being ungrateful for her nice home. But then again, it was filling up. Delphie couldn't have a bike because there was no place to put it. And their dog

Larkspur had to sleep under the kitchen table.

"Let's do it!" she said, jumping up.

Lois put her hand up like a stop sign.

"I just thought of something," she said. "We're too young. I think you have to be eighteen to buy a lottery ticket."

"Bonkers," said Daisy, falling onto the bed. The easy money had come and gone in a flash. Her little room didn't look so cozy now that she had to stay.

Daisy sighed. For a moment it had felt as though she'd already won. Her mother and her teacher warned her about her imagination. It played tricks on her. Every once in a while she thought things were real when they were not.

Daisy heard her mother's rake above her head. Now she knew what was real. A field of corn and more copper alligators.

CHAPTER 2

"I think we can get around this age thing," said Lois. "We just have to do what Mrs. Kerl tells us at school—put on our thinking caps."

The door opened and Daisy's brother Delphie bounced in. He had a baseball cap on backward and a flowerpot in his hand.

"I planted a seed in here," he said proudly. "It's going to be a tree if I water it."

"When doors are closed, you knock," said his sister sternly.

Delphie went out and shut the door. Then he knocked on it.

"Go away," said Daisy.

"That's not fair," said Delphie, sticking his head back in.

"He can come in," said Lois. "I wish I had a brother."

Delphie was eight, but sometimes he seemed younger. Because Daisy was the oldest, and went to school first, and learned to read first, and had what her parents called a "managing personality," she often felt like his mother.

Mrs. Green didn't even seem to be as handy at mothering as Daisy. Sometimes she just didn't seem to think. Like naming a boy Delphie. Delphie had started kindergarten before he found out he was named after a flower, a delphinium. The other kids called him "Belfry" and other silly names. Wouldn't you think a mother would know that?

"His eyes are the exact blue of my prize delphiniums," Mrs. Green had said when Delphie was born. Of course she would say that. Flowers ran in her family. Daisy's grandma's name was Rose, and she'd named her daughters Iris (that was Daisy's mother) and Ivy (that was Daisy's aunt). It was a family tradition now. Family legend even had it that Daisy's mother had fallen in love with her dad because his last name was Green.

Delphie came back in and set his tree on the windowsill. "If this grows into a pine tree we can decorate it at Christmas," he said.

"If we can't buy a lottery ticket, your mom and dad could buy one," said Lois, going back to their earlier conversation. "Go ask your mom. Maybe she never thought of it before."

"A lottery ticket?" said Delphie. "Let me ask!"

Before Daisy could stop him he was out the door.

"Your mom will be glad you thought of it," said Lois. "Although you should have asked her, and told her about how the house was getting too crowded and stuff. You have to use psychology with parents. You can't just blurt it out. Parents take planning."

The roof door slammed and Delphie was back.

"She says the chances of winning a lottery are one in ten trillion or something. She says it's a waste of money."

"Pooh," said Lois. "I know we'll win. What other adults do we know?"

"Miss Nelson is an adult," volunteered Delphie.

"You don't ask a librarian to buy lottery tickets for you," scoffed Daisy.

"How about my teacher?" said Delphie. "Or Aunt Ivy?"

"She's the one!" said Lois, snapping her fingers. "Your aunt Ivy will do it!"

"But then it would be Aunt Ivy's money," said Daisy.

Lois sighed. "We'll tell her she just has to buy the ticket for us. Then we'll put your mom and dad's name on it. We don't even have to tell them. It will be a surprise when they win."

That made sense, thought Daisy. Her aunt Ivy

loved to do things for her niece and nephew.

"What if Mom says she doesn't want a lottery ticket?" asked Delphie.

"She won't know about it," snapped Daisy. "It will be a secret."

"And when she wins, she won't turn down a million dollars," said Lois.

"Or two hundred," added Daisy. "Two hundred would be fine."

Lois shook her head. "Two hundred won't get you out of here," she said. "Houses probably cost ten times that much."

"Wow!" said Delphie. "Won't that be great? We'll be rich. We can buy a Christmas tree much bigger than this thing!" He waved his hand at the flowerpot on the sill.

"You'll be able to buy a million Christmas trees," said Lois. She stood up. "Let's go over to your aunt Ivy's and get this settled."

"Of course we might not win," said Daisy.

Lois waved her friend's words away with her hand. "Of course you'll win," she said. "We'll ask your aunt Ivy to buy two tickets just to be sure."

If Lois said they'd win, they'd win. She always knew what was best, thought Daisy. She was very seldom wrong.

Suddenly Daisy had another thought.

"Where do we get the money for Aunt Ivy to buy the tickets?" she asked in alarm.

"She'll lend it to you," said Lois. "Then when you win, you pay her back. Your mom won't miss a few dollars out of all that money."

How sensible Lois was! thought Daisy. Why hadn't she thought of that?

CHAPTER 3

"Aunt Ivy isn't home yet," said Delphie, looking at his watch. "She's still at work."

Aunt Ivy was a meter maid. She was the only meter maid in Liberty.

"It's a grave responsibility," she often said. "The burden of all of the meters in town falls on my shoulders." When Delphie reminded her that there weren't many meters in Liberty, she swept him aside, saying, "It's not the quantity, it's the quality." Delphie didn't know how to argue with that.

Aunt Ivy worked out of the police department. Her uniform was something like a police uniform. But instead of a badge and a number, Aunt Ivy had a small, metal parking meter on her lapel.

"Let's go down to the station and see if she's around," said Lois. "This is important business."

"We're going to see Aunt Ivy at the station," Daisy called up the stairs to her mother, who was still planting on the roof.

"Be careful," Mrs. Green called. "And don't take any wooden nickels."

"The nickels we win won't be wooden," whispered Lois, giggling on the way out.

Daisy, Delphie, and Lois hurried down the street to the police station. Sometimes Aunt Ivy was there rolling up dimes and quarters in little paper tubes. Once a week she had to empty the meters that she monitored.

"Well, look who's here," said Aunt Ivy when they walked in. "Have you got a crime or a misdemeanor to report? Fill out this form."

Though Aunt Ivy's job was limited to parking meters, law enforcement was in her blood. Many of the police officers were her friends. She couldn't resist trying to help them out when she saw the chance.

Aunt Ivy's real dream, though, was to be a private investigator. Every evening she spent long hours watching old TV series like *Columbo* and the *Rockford Files*.

"You see that man who says he's a car mechanic?" Aunt Ivy would ask the children when they came to visit, her eyes on the TV and her hand in a bowl of health-nut popcorn. "Keep your eye on him. He's no mechanic. I say he was in the stable the night of the murder."

Aunt Ivy wanted to start her own private-eye business finding people's missing loved ones, sleuthing out thieves, and capturing kidnappers and crooks who forged checks. She was going to correspondence school to learn the skills, and often took Daisy and Delphie along on the make-believe stakeouts she did as homework.

"We don't have a crime to report," said Daisy. "We want to ask a favor."

"Is it legal?" asked Aunt Ivy, sliding a row of slippery dimes into a tube. "I can't bend the law, you know. This department stands for liberty and justice for all. In Liberty, that is."

"It's perfectly legal," said Lois. "We'd like you to buy us a lottery ticket, please."

"Two," said Delphie, holding up two dirty fingers. "In case one doesn't work."

Ivy leaned back in her swivel chair and ran her hands through her blond hair. She frowned. "How old are you?" she asked.

"You know how old we are!" said Daisy. "You just gave me a birthday present!"

"I think you know what I mean," said Aunt Ivy, shaking a finger at them. "You are not eighteen."

"That's why we need you," chirped Delphie. "It's not for us; it's for my mom. It's a surprise."

"It's for my sister, is it?" said Aunt Ivy.

Daisy nodded impatiently. What was the differ-
ence? Her sister and their mom were one and the
same person!

"They need a bigger place," whispered Lois
furtively, nodding toward her friends.

"Asking an aunt to buy you a lottery ticket is
. . ." Here Aunt Ivy stopped to think.

Daisy hated unfinished sentences. "Like asking a
bus driver to take a trip?"

"No," said Aunt Ivy.

"Like asking a criminal for a loan?" asked
Delphie.

"No," said Aunt Ivy, frowning.

"Like asking a plumber to pull a tooth," said Lois.

"Exactly!" said Aunt Ivy. She threw herself back in
her chair and laughed. She laughed so hard, the
chair's wheels spun out from under her and she fell
onto the floor, sprawled on all fours.

Delphie and the girls rushed to pull her up.

A police officer at the next desk picked up the
chair.

"I don't need help," Aunt Ivy muttered.

Daisy could see that her aunt's dignity was ruffled. And she was out of breath by the time she
finally got brushed off and seated again. If her aunt
ever had to chase a crook, Daisy feared, he just
might get away.

"Well, I suppose I can help you," Aunt Ivy said. "After dinner, then. I'll get changed into civvies and meet you at Tommy Tucker's at six."

Tommy Tucker's was a gas station that sold groceries, paper plates, bubble gum, and lottery tickets.

"We'll be there," said Lois.

"Be sure you don't tell Mom or Dad," said Daisy. "It's important that it's a secret."

"I understand," said Aunt Ivy, clicking her heels together. "Your purchase is safe with me."

"One other thing," said Delphie. "We have no money. Can you lend us enough for two tickets?"

Daisy smiled her sweetest smile. "We'll pay you back when we win. I mean when Mom wins."

"It's just a dollar for a dream," said Lois politely.

Here Aunt Ivy began to laugh again. Delphie grabbed the chair and held on to it.

"Ho, ho, that's a good one," said Aunt Ivy. "Well, if I can't trust my own niece and nephew, I guess I can't trust anyone." She ruffled Delphie's hair. "I guess I can afford a couple of dollars. But I'll never see them again, you know. There is only a million to one chance of winning."

"Mrs. Green is going to win," said Lois. "I know she is."

"If she doesn't," said Daisy, "we'll pay you back on the installment plan. From our birthday money."

17

"Be there at six," said Aunt Ivy.

That evening Daisy and Delphie raced through their supper. As soon as they were finished, they met Lois and hurried the few blocks to Tommy Tucker's.

"I don't see Aunt Ivy," said Delphie.

Then they heard someone clear their throat. It was a woman wearing sunglasses and a scarf around her head. Dark hair peeped out from under the scarf. The woman had her jacket collar up around her ears.

"Pssst," she said. "Over here. It's me. I'm wearing my new disguise. I need the practice for my stake-outs."

"It's a good disguise," whispered Delphie. "I'd never know you were my aunt."

"Or a meter maid," said Lois.

Aunt Ivy stepped up to the counter. "Two please," she said in a lower voice than normal. She nodded toward the machine with the lottery tickets in it.

"Here you are, Ivy," said the clerk.

Their aunt looked upset at hearing her disguise was blown.

"Maybe I should send this outfit back and order another," she grumbled. "One with a mustache and black wig."

They all went outside. Aunt Ivy took a pencil out of her purse and leaned on a gas pump to write. She printed IRIS GREEN in big neat letters on the tickets.

"Just to be sure these don't fall into the wrong hands," she said, "put them in a safe place till the drawing. It's Friday night."

Today was Wednesday, thought Daisy. How were they going to get through forty-eight hours of waiting time? And where was a good place to hide the tickets? Her mother came into their rooms to clean or collect dirty clothes. This was a big secret, one that would make them all rich. They had to find a safe, safe place.

CHAPTER 4

"I know where we can hide them!" shouted Delphie on the way home. "I'll put them in my shoe!"

He sat down on the sidewalk and took off his sneaker.

"Ick!" said Lois, holding her nose. "They'll get all wrinkled and worn out and smelly."

"I'll put them in my library book for now," said Aunt Ivy. She took the tickets and slipped them in between the pages of *The Role of the Modern Meter Maid in Liberty Law Enforcement*.

"They will be clean and flat and safe right here between pages 102 and 103." Aunt Ivy slipped the book back into her tote bag.

"Now," she went on. "Let's celebrate. I'll buy you all a carrot-juice cocktail."

Delphie made a face. He hated carrot juice. But he couldn't be rude to someone who was making them rich. He and the girls trooped behind Aunt Ivy to the health-food bar.

"Four Rabbit Rousers," said Aunt Ivy, flinging four dollars down on the counter.

Aunt Ivy was into health food. She ate granola for breakfast and sprouts for lunch and tofu for dinner. In between she took vitamin tablets for her skin and ginkgo so her limbs wouldn't ache and black currant oil for her memory. "What's a private eye without a good memory?" she often said.

When Aunt Ivy wasn't looking, Delphie poured his Rabbit Rouser onto a nearby ficus plant.

"You'll kill it!" whispered Daisy.

"If rabbits and people drink it, it can't kill a plant!" he whispered back.

Aunt Ivy drained her glass, smacked her lips, and said, "Now we just wait and see what happens on Friday."

Friday seemed ages away to Daisy. When she got home she put a red X on her calendar on The Day. Then she and Lois and Delphie tried to keep busy. They ran errands for their mothers and cleaned their rooms and rode bikes down country roads and dried the dishes and cleaned the birdcage and walked Larkspur and brushed his hair. And still it was only Thursday.

"What we should be doing is packing your things," said Lois on Thursday afternoon. "For the big move."

"Not yet," said Daisy. "My mom and dad don't even know they're moving. And we haven't sold this house yet, and we don't have a new one to move into."

Lois waved a hand as if that didn't matter. "You will have one soon, and we could save time by packing now." She glanced around at all the knickknacks and dishes and end tables. And all the plants and metal garden animals.

Daisy knew her mother wouldn't like it one bit if they started taking plates out of the cupboard and chairs out from under the table, with no explanation. Speed wasn't everything. But Lois was both smart and efficient. She was organized and level-headed. And Daisy knew she would not be satisfied until she got *something* into a suitcase.

The girls went into Daisy's room and Daisy took old things that she did not wear anymore off her closet shelf. She took down toys she'd outgrown. Then she took out the blue suitcase she used when she went to stay overnight with Aunt Ivy. Lois tumbled the things into it and shut the lid. Daisy put it in the back of her closet where her mother wouldn't see it and ask questions.

"What's next?" asked Lois, brushing off her jeans, as if Daisy's room was a dirty place to work.

"It's almost suppertime," said Daisy.

"I'd better get home!" said Lois. "We're going to my grandma's for dinner. But I'll see you tomorrow at three o'clock. Right here. We'll watch them draw your mom's number on TV."

"I'll be waiting," said Daisy. "So will Delphie."

That night at suppertime, Daisy and Delphie had trouble keeping the big news to themselves. Daisy wanted to shout, "Have we got a surprise for you! And it isn't even your birthday!"

Mrs. Green chattered on about the lack of rain and the price of some new rosebush called Olivia.

"Just one bush is more than twenty dollars!" she said. "That's how spectacular it is!"

Delphie blurted out, "Tomorrow you'll be able to buy lots of . . ."

Daisy clapped her hand over Delphie's mouth. Her parents looked up at her in surprise.

"I thought I saw a fly," said Daisy. "It was going to land on Delphie's nose."

"I didn't see a fly," said Mr. Green, taking some salad. "Did you see a fly, Iris?"

"They sneak in here every now and then," Mrs. Green said. "I believe there's a hole in the screen. Now what were you saying, Delphie, about my getting lots of something?"

"Pots, not lots," said Daisy. "He said you'd be able to buy pots tomorrow."

"Pots to put plants in," said Delphie loudly.

His mother frowned. "I don't need more pots," she said. "I have pots. What I need is rosebushes. And I want Olivia."

Daisy and Delphie concentrated on chewing and not talking. If they talked, the surprise might come out.

"That was a fine meal," said Mr. Green with a sigh of satisfaction when they finished. "There's nothing like a good supper at home with one's family."

Daisy looked at her father and mother. They seemed so happy. So satisfied. Maybe it was a mistake to uproot them and move to a bigger house.

Still, thought Daisy, a metal llama was looking over her dad's shoulder even as they ate, and if Delphie got up quickly he would bump smack into the three-piece alligator. No, it was definitely a good thing to win the lottery. It had to be.

Daisy and Delphie helped their parents clear the table. Her mother chattered on about Olivia and their father showed them a newspaper ad for a new metal cutter that could make his sculpturing easier.

"That's my dream," he said, tapping the paper.

"A dream for a dollar!" said Delphie.

"It's more than a dollar," laughed Mr. Green while Daisy glared at Delphie. She was tired of getting him out of tight situations.

When the dishes were done, Daisy and Delphie watched TV and then got ready for bed. "Won't it be great when they win and Dad can get piles of metal cutters?" said Delphie.

"And Mom can get all the Olivias she wants!" agreed Daisy.

Once in bed, though, Daisy's stomach began to ache, and she knew it was not from her mother's good dinner. It was from excitement.

Or was it worry?

CHAPTER 5

"Your dad and I are going to the city to shop," said Mrs. Green the next afternoon. "They have a special on organic fertilizer at Belson's. Do you and Delphie want to come along? You could use some new sneakers."

Daisy shook her head. Usually she would jump at the chance to go to town. It meant they would eat at Roundup Ron's, where your burger came with a little lasso around it. "Not today," she said. "Delphie and I will be fine. We have things to do."

Mrs. Green frowned. "Don't talk to strangers or touch matches," she said.

Her mother watched too much TV, thought Daisy. There was hardly ever a stranger in Liberty, and she and Delphie never touched matches. Daisy didn't even think they owned any.

"There is fruit salad in the refrigerator," Mrs. Green went on. "And tuna fish. I'll ask Mr. Wong to look in now and then to see that you are all right. We'll only be gone an hour or so."

"Okay," said Daisy. "But can Lois come over?"

When her parents left, Daisy felt a great sense of power, even though Mr. Wong would be looking in on them. Anyway, she was the oldest, so the responsibility was hers. And it meant they could watch the lottery drawing uninterrupted. Though on the other hand, when they won it would be nice if her parents were there to get the news immediately.

By two-thirty Daisy was in front of the TV set waiting. She put chips and soda pop on the squid-shaped coffee table her dad had made. The little suction cups along the squid's legs made nice holders for glasses or pop cans. Daisy often wondered why her father didn't sell more squid tables, but they were not one of his more popular items.

"It's time!" shouted Delphie, slamming the door on his way in. "I hope Aunt Ivy is watching."

"She can't watch TV at work," said Daisy. "We can call her after the drawing." She turned on the television.

There was a rap on the door. Daisy opened it, and Lois came in.

"Have you got the tickets?" she demanded.

Delphie looked at Daisy. Daisy put her hand over her mouth.

"Aunt Ivy has them!" she said. "In her library book!"

On TV a man was spinning a big basket with numbers in it.

"I know the numbers on our tickets," said Delphie. "They are 45802 and 45803." He frowned. "Or maybe it's 48502."

"I think both the numbers had a 7 in them," said Daisy.

"It doesn't matter," said Lois. "We will write the winning number down and get the tickets afterward. We just check them, and then take them to Tommy Tucker's."

Daisy relaxed. It would be okay. Lois said so.

The man on TV stopped spinning the basket. His mouth was moving but there was no sound.

"Turn it up," said Lois.

Delphie turned the knob. Nothing happened. "It's as loud as it can go!" he said.

"What's the matter with your set?" said Lois. "We won't hear the winning number!"

"Sometimes it takes awhile to warm up," said Daisy, giving the volume button a poke.

They waited. The woman who was to draw the lottery number came on the stage. She smiled and said a lot of words but none that they could hear. The basket was turning.

Lois stood up. "We're going to miss it!" she yelled.

Just then a commercial for dog biscuits came on. Larkspur wandered in to watch it.

"We have about one minute to find a TV set that works!" said Lois. "Let's go over to my house."

Lois dashed out the door and down the steps. Daisy raced up to Mr. Wong's to explain where they were going. And then she and Delphie tore after Lois. Lois did not live far away, but it was bound to take more than a minute. Larkspur sniffed the TV screen, found out the food was not real, and followed them.

After greeting Mrs. Fable in panting voices, Daisy, Delphie, and Lois ran to Lois's room. Lois had her own TV set on her dresser, a little white one. She turned it on. It lit up. It had sound! It had a picture! But the woman on the screen was saying, "Good luck, and tune in next Friday so we can make you a millionaire!" Then the dog food came back. This time Larkspur didn't even lift a whisker.

Daisy stamped her foot. "Leaping lizards!" she said. "What do we do now?"

"It's all right," said Lois. "We know we won. We just have to get the tickets from your aunt Ivy and take them in. They'll announce the number again on the news."

"Well, let's call Aunt Ivy," said Delphie.

Lois picked up the little white phone by her bed. Daisy dialed the number.

"Aunt Ivy, please," she said.

"Ivy's not in today," said a gruff voice. "She's in St. Paul at a seminar on canine assistance for the private eye."

CHAPTER 6

"St. Paul?" shouted Daisy. "She's in St. Paul today?"

"I'm sorry," said the voice on the other end.

Daisy felt cross. Aunt Ivy had either forgotten the drawing, or the meeting. She was easily distracted, is what she was, thought Daisy. After all, she was the one who said, "Now we will just wait for Friday." How could she say to wait for Friday and then go out of town?

"There's no time to lose," said Lois. "Maybe we should take a bus to St. Paul and find her."

Their mother would not approve of them taking a bus to St. Paul, thought Daisy. And how would they find Aunt Ivy even if they got there? She could already be on her way home.

"The early news is on in ten minutes," said Daisy. "Let's get the winning number and write it down."

Lois turned the TV back on and the three of them sat on Lois's bed to watch.

"Rain floods streets in Columbus," said a man

with no hair.

"Robbers steal artwork from local museum," said a lady with a suntan.

"Those PIs better get canine assistance in a hurry," said Delphie. "Dogs could sniff some paintings and then run and catch those guys."

"All this news—and the number of the winning lottery ticket—coming up in just a moment," the bald man said with a big smile.

Lois's mother stuck her head in the door. "Almost dinnertime," she said. "Would you two like to stay and eat with us?"

"Thank you very much, but my mother will be expecting us home," said Daisy before Delphie could race to the table and tie the napkin around his neck. "We'll be leaving in a minute."

"Well, you're welcome to stay," said Lois's mother warmly before she left.

The bald man talked about the floods. He talked about the stolen artwork. Then there was another commercial. Then at last, the woman with the suntan said, "And now for that winning lottery number!" She read the number out loud. At the same time it flashed onto the screen: 45707.

"If you hold this winning ticket, bring it in and claim a windfall!"

"We don't want wind!" shouted Delphie. "We want money!"

"A windfall is money!" said Lois.

Daisy wrote down the winning number.

"Now all we need are our tickets," said Lois. "And the money is ours."

"Is it one of our numbers?" asked Daisy.

"Of course it's one of our numbers," said Lois. She put her hands on her hips in disgust. "I told you we'd win, didn't I? We could collect it right now, but I suppose they want the ticket. There are always a lot of silly rules."

"We have to go home," said Daisy, pulling Delphie up off the bed. "Mom and Dad will be looking for us."

"We can go to Aunt Ivy's after supper," said Delphie. "We can eat fast."

When Daisy and Delphie got home, their father was broiling fish in the kitchen. He had a big white apron on and something smelled just a little burned.

"Wouldn't it be nice to have a cook?" asked Delphie, setting the table with their old dishes. Some of the plates had chips out of them. "And get new dishes and stuff?"

Mrs. Green looked at her son. "Since when is there something the matter with our dishes?" She laughed. "Or with your father's cooking for that matter?"

"There isn't," chirped Delphie, "but if we had a cook Dad could do other stuff."

Mr. and Mrs. Green looked puzzled. Daisy put silverware around the table.

"Is this stuff real silver?" she asked.

"Why, no," said her mother. "It's stainless steel."

"It gets the food to our mouths just as well as silver," said Mr. Green. He proved his point by spearing a bit of fish with his fork. "See?"

"But it's bent," said Delphie. "And this spoon has a dent in it."

"Have you two been to the Vanderbilts for dinner lately?" laughed their mother.

Daisy didn't know who the Vanderbilts were. She could tell by his face that Delphie didn't either. Lois would, she thought.

"I'll bet you've been reading library books about the movie stars, or rock stars," said Mr. Green. "That's where you're getting these highfalutin ideas."

"Still," mused Mrs. Green, "I'd like some good silver one day. And some dishes with no cracks."

"When our ship comes in," said Mr. Green, putting his arm around his wife.

Delphie tried to wink at Daisy about the ship coming in, but he couldn't keep one eye open and one closed. Instead he blinked with both eyes.

"Do you have something in your eye, dear?" asked his mother.

"He's just tired out from his busy day," said Mr. Green.

They sat down at the table, and Mrs. Green passed Daisy the baked beans.

"Why do we have beans all the time?" asked Delphie.

"They are very good for you," said their mother. "They are nutritious, nourishing, and on sale at Rooney's."

"Pretty soon we might be able to buy things that aren't on sale," said Daisy, trying to sound mysterious. "Like lobster and those green things Lois's mother gets in little jars. Somebody's heart."

"I don't want to eat somebody's heart!" said Delphie, grabbing his chest and making gagging noises. "Even when we're rich. I mean if we're rich."

Daisy shot a warning look at Delphie. They did not want to give away the surprise, now that it was getting so close.

"I think you mean artichoke hearts," said their father. "They aren't real hearts. Just the heart of the plant. And what's all this talk about rich tonight?"

"Nothing," said Daisy quickly. "I mean just in case. Someday. When you sell all your garden animals."

During dessert, the phone rang. Mrs. Green answered it.

"Why, Ivy, you're back from your seminar," she said.

Daisy and Delphie looked at each other. Then they gobbled down the last of their bread pudding, and said, "Excuse me," as they bolted out of their chairs.

"We've got to see Aunt Ivy!" called Daisy

"We'll be back before dark!" Delphie shouted.

"I'll dry the dishes as soon as we get home," Daisy added.

"That will be the last time for either of us to do dishes," whispered Delphie as they hurried out the door. "By tomorrow I bet we have an electric dishwasher!"

CHAPTER 7

Daisy and Delphie ran around the block to Lois's as fast as they could and rang the doorbell.

"She's back!" shouted Daisy. "Aunt Ivy's back!"

Lois came out with a milk mustache and her mouth full of chocolate cake.

"I didn't have time to wash up," she said, wiping her face with a Kleenex.

"That's okay," said Delphie. "We can wash *after* we win the money."

The three of them dashed down the street past the police station, the library, and Tommy Tucker's. They reached Aunt Ivy's and pounded on her apartment door. They pounded so loudly that several of the neighbors looked out into the hall to see what was going on.

When Aunt Ivy finally opened her door, she seemed surprised to see them.

"What's up?" she asked. "Your mother didn't

mention you were coming over. I just got in the door myself a short time ago."

"Do you know what day this is?" demanded Daisy.

Aunt Ivy stopped to think. "It is Friday. The day of my canine meeting in St. Paul."

"Wrong," said Daisy, deepening her voice like a disappointed game-show host.

Aunt Ivy pointed to her calendar. Sure enough, the meeting was written in red ink.

Daisy stamped her foot. Delphie sighed. Lois stood by politely because only relatives can get cross with each other in public.

"Is there an eclipse?" asked Aunt Ivy, rushing to the window. "No," she said, tapping her forehead, "I'll bet it's the night Dr. Lean is speaking about antioxidants on channel two!" She rushed to the TV and turned it on.

"It is not Dr. Lean," said Daisy. "Friday is the lottery drawing! We need to have the tickets to get the money."

"Oh," said Aunt Ivy. She gave them the kind of smile adults sometimes give children. It means children are too young to be smart, thought Daisy.

"You know," Aunt Ivy said gently, "you should not get your hopes so high. The odds are a million to one against winning the lottery."

Aunt Ivy did not believe them! She didn't realize that when Lois said they would win, they would win. What kind of aunt wouldn't trust her niece? And her niece's friend?

"Just give us the tickets," pleaded Daisy.

"Well, all right, but don't get overexcited now," said Aunt Ivy. She picked up papers and dishes from the table. "Let's see now, where did we put those tickets?"

Lois rolled her eyes at Daisy. "You put them in a book," she said.

"A library book," said Daisy.

"*The Role of the Modern Meter Maid in Liberty Law Enforcement*," said Delphie.

"Well, it's around here someplace," said Aunt Ivy, turning over more books and papers. "I think it was blue."

"I think it was red," said Daisy.

"Mauve," said Lois. "It was a mauve color."

The others looked at her. What in the world was mauve?

"This color," said Lois, pointing to her sneakers.

"That's pink," said Delphie.

Lois shook her head. "It's more of a rose shade," she said.

Why in the world were they arguing over color, Daisy wondered, when they needed to find those tickets!

"Look in the kitchen," said Aunt Ivy. "Then we'll try the bedroom. I often read in bed."

Daisy lifted coffee cups and newspapers and private-eye magazines.

Delphie looked behind chairs and under tables.

Lois looked under Aunt Ivy's bed, and in the cabinet with her vitamins, protein powders, and herbs.

Aunt Ivy sat down in the lotus position and meditated. She said she had to see the book in her mind, visualize it, and then she could walk right to it.

"Think," said Daisy. "Think hard, Aunt Ivy."

"You can't force it," breathed her aunt. "You simply have to will it forth and wait until the message arrives."

A moment later, she cried, "It's come! That book was due at the library. I dropped it off on the way back to town tonight."

Delphie hit his head with his hand. Why couldn't Aunt Ivy have overdue books like everyone else?

Aunt Ivy tried to jump up and tripped over one foot that would not come unlotused. Delphie gave it a pull and she was on her feet.

"The library is closed," said Lois.

Aunt Ivy nodded. "It was closed when I brought

the book back," she said. "I had to put it in the box outside."

"Maybe it's still there!" said Daisy.

The children rushed out the door, leaving Aunt Ivy behind in her bathrobe.

"Wait!" she called. "Come back!"

But they were too far away by then to hear her. They were already turning the corner to the library. There by the main door was the box for returned books. It was metal with a large drop slot to put the books in.

"Your whole future is in that box," whispered Lois dramatically. "Sealed up so we can't get at it. By the time the library opens tomorrow it may be too late."

Delphie kicked the box. "We have to get it out," he said.

"We can't," said Daisy. "Even if we could fit in that chute, it's illegal."

"It isn't as though we want to steal the book," said Lois. "What do we want with *The Role of the Modern Meter Maid in Liberty Law Enforcement*? We don't want their dumb old books. Those are our tickets and we're entitled to them."

What Lois said made sense. It could not be illegal to claim your very own lottery tickets that were paid for and had your parents' names on them.

Daisy looked around. No one was nearby. People were probably eating dinner and watching the news. And there was a big bush in front of the book box that hid it from the street.

"That slot is about the size of Delphie's head," said Lois. "It makes sense for him to try to reach the book. Neither one of us will fit."

"I'm going in for it!" shouted Delphie. A moment later, he had his arms and shoulders in the chute. He hung there like a pair of jeans on their mother's clothesline.

Soon he was in up to his waist. His feet were up in the air kicking and flailing. Suddenly Daisy had a terrible thought. Even if Delphie got in, how would he get out? What if he got stuck in the middle, like Pooh Bear in Rabbit's hole? What if they had to hang towels on Delphie's north end for the rest of his life?

Suddenly she heard what she'd been dreading.

"I'm stuck!" called Delphie. "My belt is caught on the chute!" His voice sounded like it was coming from a basement or a deep, deep hole.

The girls pulled and tugged but could not get him loose. He couldn't push farther in, and he couldn't pull out. Daisy felt like crying.

"Can you reach the book?" called Lois, thinking of more practical things.

"I can feel some books, but it's too dark to see what they are," Delphie's hollow voice called back.

"Pick them up, one at a time, and flip through them for the tickets," said Lois, speaking clearly and carefully like a teacher. "You know what tickets feel like."

"There's too many," whined Delphie. "And I'm getting dizzy hanging like this."

"We're talking about your *life!*" said Lois firmly. "This is no time to think about your circulation. You can feel the tickets even if you're dizzy."

Daisy thought Lois was being a bit insensitive, but she knew her friend was right. It was now or never.

"Think of the dishwasher, Delph," she called supportively. "Think of having room for a bike."

The girls could hear Delphie thrashing around in the box. *Bang, bonk, slap* went the books as Delphie took Lois's orders.

Flip, flop, conk went more books. Delphie's feet waved wildly.

"How are we going to get him out of here, even if he does find the tickets?" Daisy asked. She felt herself getting tearful again.

"First things first," said Lois. "As soon as we get the tickets, we'll worry about that. That's step two."

"Hey!" shouted Delphie suddenly. "I think I've got them!"

"Don't lose them!" shouted Lois. "Put them in your pocket or somewhere safe."

"I can't reach my pocket!" shouted Delphie. "Get me out of here!"

"We will," said Daisy, trying to sound confident. Lois would find a way. She was the smartest one here. And besides, she was the one who got them into this in the first place. If Delphie had to live in a book box the rest of his life, it would be Lois's fault.

Lois examined the box. "The top doesn't come off," she announced. "It has screws in it, so no one can steal books."

The girls pulled on Delphie's feet as hard as they could, but he screamed so loud they had to stop.

"Stop!" said Lois. "People will think we're killing him!"

The girls sat down on the library steps to think.

"I guess we have to go for help," said Lois. "There's no other way."

Daisy could not believe her friend had let her down. Going for help meant they could be arrested. Aunt Ivy had once told her library books were government property. And the government didn't mess around with criminals. It locked them up.

But they didn't have to surrender to the government. The government came to them. When the girls looked up, they saw two police officers pulling up in a squad car. The police got out of the car, and one of them said, "What's going on here?" in a voice that didn't sound friendly at all.

CHAPTER 8

The police officers came closer. They stared at Delphie's legs coming out of the book-box slot. One of them whistled a low whistle like he didn't believe what he was seeing.

He tapped the box. "Why is he in there?" he asked.

"He fell in," said Lois.

Daisy knew the police would not buy that.

"Tampering with public property is an illegal act," said the officer, taking out a clipboard and pen.

Daisy wondered if having a meter maid for an aunt would carry any weight with the police. But even if it did help, Aunt Ivy would be humiliated to have her own relatives turn out to be common criminals. She may even lose her job! Daisy had a sudden picture in her mind of her whole family behind bars (except for Delphie who was living in the book box). She saw them growing old, eating bread and water instead of turkey for Thanksgiving dinner.

"Tell me your names," said the first officer, who had "Slater" on his shirt. "Then we'll try to get him out of that box."

"I'm Lois," said Lois, "and these are my friends, Daisy and Delphinium."

"Your real names," said Officer Slater crossly.

"Those are our real names!" shouted Delphie from inside the book box. "We are named after flowers."

The girls just smiled sweetly.

Officer Slater went to the squad car and got some tools. He carefully unscrewed the top of the book box and lifted it off. The police were very helpful, Daisy had to admit. She and Lois would never have gotten Delphie out.

Delphie crawled out over the side of the box. He had a red mark on his cheek and Daisy thought his head looked flat from standing on it. She hoped it was just her imagination.

"Are you all right, sonny?" Officer Slater asked.

"I guess so," said Delphie, rubbing his head.

"Let's all get in the car," said Officer Slater.

"In movies cops give kids ice cream when they arrest them," whispered Lois as they rode in the police car.

There was no ice cream. Instead, Officer Slater asked for their phone number and called the Greens.

"Let's try and escape!" whispered Delphie. "We can run faster than they can."

"No," said Daisy. She could see the headlines, BOOK-BOX THIEVES ESCAPE. APB OUT FOR THEIR CAPTURE. LARGE REWARD FOR ANY CLUES LEADING TO THEIR CONVICTION.

Daisy looked around. What was Lois doing? She was the cause of all this. Why wasn't she finding a way out? All she seemed to be doing was trying on a pair of handcuffs she found on the desk.

Daisy did not know what her parents said on the phone, but before long they were both at the door with Aunt Ivy.

"We have apprehended these small mischief makers," said Officer Slater, pointing his thumb toward them.

Aunt Ivy was frowning. So were the Greens. The officer explained the situation, and then Lois spoke up.

"We had to look for the book," she said. "It was a matter of life or death."

Daisy looked at her.

"Well, almost," Lois said. "It was a very important matter."

Aunt Ivy held up her hand. "It's all my fault. I had no idea they were going to the library."

"What book was so important that Delphie had to dive into the box for it?" asked Mrs. Green. "What book couldn't wait till morning?"

"*The Role of the Modern Meter Maid in Liberty Law Enforcement*," said Lois.

Now the police officers looked really baffled.

Then Aunt Ivy explained about the lottery tickets. When she finished, everyone laughed and agreed it was a harmless motive. The officers warned the children about mistreating public property, and then released them.

On the way home Aunt Ivy lectured them about taking the law into their own hands. "This could have been a serious infraction of the law," she warned.

"To say nothing of an infraction of Delphie's head," said Mr. Green.

"And no tickets are worth all this fuss," said Mrs. Green. "I'm afraid lottery tickets are a waste of Aunt Ivy's money."

Delphie opened his mouth to disagree, but Daisy whispered into his ear. "Don't tell them yet!" she said. "We have to get the money first."

"All's well that ends well," said their father. "But

if you want something again that you can't reach, it's best to ask us."

As soon as they got home, Lois, Daisy, and Delphie went to Daisy's room and shut the door.

"Do you have them?" demanded Lois.

Delphie smiled. In all the excitement no adult had thought to ask about the tickets. Delphie reached into his pocket and held them up.

Lois took the winning number out of her jeans pocket. She held it up next to their two tickets. The first ticket did not match. Lois threw it into Daisy's wastebasket.

But the other ticket said 45707 on it very clearly.

"You see?" said Lois, without surprise. "I told you you would win."

Daisy could not believe her eyes. Even though she trusted Lois, she was surprised.

"I have to use the phone," said Lois, heading out into the hall. She picked up the receiver and dialed the number of Tommy Tucker's.

"Hello," she said politely. "I hope it isn't too late, but we won the lottery and need to come in and collect the money. Is now a good time? And do you have a bag to put it in, or do we bring our own?"

Even from where she sat, Daisy could hear laughter on the other end of the phone line. "Some kids

think they won the lottery!" a man guffawed.

"I don't like your attitude," said Lois sternly. "I have the winning ticket right here. It says 45707 on it."

"Sure it does," Daisy could hear the man say. "Now listen, little lady. The telephone isn't something to play games with. And children can't win the lottery. I'll bet you didn't know that, did you?"

Lois stamped her foot on the hall floor. "Of course I know that," she said. "It is Mr. and Mrs. Green's ticket and they are not children. They will be in with the ticket to pick up the money. So you better have it ready."

Lois slammed down the phone.

"It sure is a lot of work to win the lottery," said Delphie, sighing.

"I think it's time to tell my parents," Daisy said. "After all, it's their money."

Just then the phone rang. Daisy answered. It was Lois's mother wanting her to come home.

"I'll see you guys later," Lois said. "By that time you should be rich."

Then she waved and ran out the door.

Daisy picked up the ticket with 45707 on it. She stood it up on her dresser under the light of her little lamp. Just a little piece of cardboard with numbers on it, thought Daisy. Just a little, tiny piece of cardboard that was stuck in a library book at the bottom of a book box.

But Daisy had the feeling that this little piece of cardboard was going to change her life from this day forward. For better or worse—words she'd heard on TV weddings. And Daisy hated change.

Well, it was too late now. She picked up the ticket and turned to Delphie.

"Here goes," she said. "It's time to tell Mom and Dad the news."

CHAPTER 9

Mr. Green was bending wires to make a mold for reindeer antlers. The TV was on and he was glancing at *Supernatural Tales* as he worked.

"See that girl, Daisy? She spotted two UFOs in a field by her house and no one believes her." Mr. Green chuckled.

Mrs. Green was looking through seed catalogs. On the table in front of her was a magazine open to an article on root rot.

It was a perfect family, thought Daisy, even if they didn't have a lot of money. Why did Lois think they needed more money? Daisy had forgotten the reason. It had made sense to her then. Now it didn't. If it hadn't been for Lois, she and Delphie would be in their little beds, cozy and warm, with the sound of loving voices (and the tales of the supernatural) humming in the living room nearby. They would be dreaming nonlottery dreams and their lives would stay the same.

Mrs. Green looked up. "Isn't it almost bedtime?" she asked.

"We have something to tell you!" said Delphie. He had waited a long time for this moment.

"What is it, dear?" asked Mrs. Green.

Delphie waved the lottery ticket. Daisy took a deep breath.

"Remember the lottery tickets Aunt Ivy told you about?" she asked. "The ones that were in the library book Delphie got out of the book box?"

"Those things," said Mr. Green. "Not a chance in the world of winning the lottery."

"Yes, there is!" said Delphie.

"We bought the ticket for you, and you won," said Daisy. "You owe Aunt Ivy two dollars. But you don't have to pay her yet. You can pay her out of the money you collect."

"We had to borrow the money to get the tickets," said Delphie. "It was Lois's idea."

Daisy and Delphie stopped talking and waited for their parents to say something.

But Mr. and Mrs. Green just stared at them.

"I'm sorry," said Daisy. Her parents seemed to be in shock. "I know we shouldn't have gone ahead without asking you, but Lois said we needed a bigger house and Aunt Ivy bought the tickets for us because we aren't old enough, and we put your name on them, and well, we thought it would be a nice surprise."

Still her parents just stared at them. It made Daisy nervous. Shock was not good for old people. Excitement could even make their heart stop! She would give them another five minutes, and then she'd call 911.

Supernatural Tales droned on.

Finally Mrs. Green found her voice.

"People in Liberty don't win the lottery," she said. "Sometimes it's easy to confuse what we imagine and what is real. You probably dreamed we won."

Delphie was shaking his head. But his mother went on.

"Dreams can be so real that even in broad daylight you think they're true. Why the other night I dreamed we had a home in the country. But when I woke up, here I was in Liberty, the same as always, with my feet on the ground."

"That's right," said Mr. Green. "Why sometimes my sculptures look so real I think they could bite me! But of course I know they can't."

He shook his finger playfully at Daisy and Delphie. "We'll pay Aunt Ivy her two dollars," he said. "But you children must try not to make things up like this again, do you hear?"

"It wasn't a dream," said Daisy, "and we didn't make it up."

"You really won!" said Delphie. "All you have to do is take the ticket in to Tommy Tucker's and collect the money."

"Well, I can settle this easily, once and for all," said Mr. Green, picking up the telephone and dialing a number.

"Hello, Tommy Tucker's? Could you tell me what the winning lottery number is, please?" Mr. Green listened to the reply. "Thank you very much," he said. He hung up the phone. "Now," he said. "The winning number is 45707."

He walked over to Delphie and took the ticket from his hand. He read it out loud. "See, this ticket says 45707."

Mrs. Green went over and looked at the ticket herself. Then she sat down. Her face was white.

Daisy couldn't tell if her parents were upset about all the money, or pleased.

But as Daisy watched, a slow smile spread over her mother's face.

Then a smile spread over her father's face.

And then suddenly Mr. Green picked up the wire antlers and tossed them into the air. They caught on a light fixture and hung there like a tree ornament!

Mrs. Green picked up a pile of seed catalogs and tossed them into the air, too! They came back down fluttering and falling like giant snowflakes.

"We won!" she shouted. "We actually won the lottery!"

"YAHOO!" shouted Mr. Green. He began to chase his wife around the living room, weaving in and out among the garden animals and slipping and sliding on the seed catalogs.

Now it was Daisy and Delphie who were quiet. Their parents had gone crazy!

Suddenly Mr. Green swooped down and grabbed Daisy's hand. Then he grabbed Delphie's hand. The four of them made a circle and spun around in a dance until they were dizzy.

"We won because we won because we won because we won!" sang Mr. Green.

"We won because we won because weeeee won because we won!" they joined in.

It was the song they sang at the stadium after ball games. That is, they sang it when Liberty won the game!

Even though Daisy was still confused, she couldn't help getting swept up in the excitement. Neither could Delphie.

Finally the family collapsed on the floor,

laughing and singing until Mr. Wong knocked on the door to see what was the matter. When they told him, he ran to get his wife. Then they came in and began to laugh and sing, too.

"We should have known that Daisy wouldn't make something up!" said her father, giving her a hug.

Her mother came and put her arms around Daisy and Delphie and squeezed them. She had tears in her eyes.

"I didn't even say thank you," she said. "Thank you for this monumental gift."

"You're welcome," said Delphie.

The whole family began to laugh again.

"I have to call Ivy," said Mrs. Green at last.

The phone rang at Aunt Ivy's for a long time. When her aunt finally answered, Daisy could hear her yawn into the phone.

"I'm sorry I woke you, Ivy," her mother said.

Then she told her the good news. "Can you imagine that?" cried Mrs. Green.

Aunt Ivy must have said something like children like to pretend, and Daisy has a wild imagination, and the odds are very slim, because their mother said, "But we won, Ivy! We really won! We called Tommy Tucker's!"

Her mother hung up the phone. "She doesn't believe us!" laughed Mrs. Green.

"Imagine that!" said Mr. Green, winking at Daisy.

When the Wongs left, Delphie dozed off on the davenport.

Daisy was relieved to see her parents so happy. Maybe things would not have to change too much.

"How much money did we win?" she asked her dad cautiously. "Two hundred dollars?"

"As far as I can figure," said her dad, "it is more than ten million dollars!"

Ten million dollars! Daisy couldn't even count that high! That was enough to buy more than one home!

Her father got out his calculator. "We'll owe a lot of it in taxes," he said. "Still, what's left will be plenty!"

He laughed and ruffled Daisy's hair.

Mrs. Green was already drawing up plans for a greenhouse.

"In a greenhouse I can raise things that like humidity," she said. "Why, someday we could even have a farm, and raise squash and potatoes and beans to sell! We could get a truck and take things to market!"

Suddenly Aunt Ivy burst in the door. Her hair was disheveled and Daisy could see her nightgown peeping out from under her shirt.

"You won the lottery!" she shouted, grabbing her sister and dancing around the living room. "Number 45707 is the winning number!"

Daisy had never seen a meter maid dance before. And she had never seen her aunt this playful.

"I say we get down to Tommy Tucker's with that ticket right now!" said Aunt Ivy.

"In the middle of the night?" said Delphie, waking up and rubbing his eyes.

"Of course!" said Mr. Green.

"This calls for Rabbit Rousers all around, my treat!" said Aunt Ivy.

Daisy and Delphie moaned. The one thing they didn't need on an excited stomach was a Rabbit Rouser!

And the one person who should really be celebrating with them, thought Daisy, was sound asleep at home in her own little bed. If it hadn't been for Lois, they would not be drinking Rabbit Rousers in the middle of the night!

But Lois had known that they would win from the very beginning. It was no surprise to her!

CHAPTER 10

"Lois should really come, too," said Daisy. "It was her idea."

Mr. Green looked at his watch. "I don't think we should wake her at this hour," he said.

So the whole Green family rushed to Tommy Tucker's.

When Mr. Green handed the ticket to the man behind the counter, the man scratched his head and his eyes got wide.

"Well I'll be darned," he said. "You really did win. You must be the Greens that have been calling. Hey folks," he called to the other customers. "We've got a lottery winner here in Liberty! Right here in Tommy Tucker's!"

Daisy was surprised to see how many people were in a convenience store at night. People were buying newspapers and gas for their cars and milk and whipping cream and packages of chocolate cupcakes with pink frosting on them. One lady had a cart full of disposable diapers and cans of formula. Daisy didn't see a baby, and she hoped it was home asleep.

Word of the winners got around the store fast, and suddenly all of the shoppers who were in line to pay now got in line to shake the Greens' hands.

"I'm thrilled, simply thrilled!" said Mrs. Kerl, Daisy's teacher, running up with a barbecued chicken in her basket. She threw her arms around Daisy in a hug. "But we mustn't think this means we don't need a good education," she went on, shaking her finger at her student. "Money can't buy wisdom." Mrs. Kerl tapped her forehead.

"Well, yes it can, Mrs. Kerl," laughed Mr. Green. "Money can help buy education, when it comes to college tuition."

Mrs. Kerl waved Mr. Green's words away with her hand. "Oh, you're teasing now, you funny man! But you can't put a price on education!"

Then Miss Nelson, the librarian, came over and told Delphie that he'd now be able to afford the fines on his overdue books!

"I paid those!" said Delphie to his dad. "What's she talking about?"

"That's just a little lottery humor," explained his father. "People like to make money jokes at a time like this."

Daisy guessed that this was only the first of many things they'd have to get used to.

Tommy must have been busy on the phone, because now the man from the *Liberty Bugle* had arrived. At his side was Miss Parsons, the photographer, already snapping pictures of the family.

"Now all of you, stand back so I can get the winners!" she said, climbing up on a chair to get a good shot. Aunt Ivy pushed Daisy and Delphie up front, and she herself stood between their parents. Daisy noticed she had her meter-maid pin on the front of her shirt, even though it was after hours and no money was needed in the parking meters.

"I think the whole town is here," laughed Mr. Green.

Just as he said that, Daisy saw Lois come in with her family!

"What are you doing here so late?" asked Daisy. "Is it on the news already?"

Lois shook her head. "We went to a movie and we stopped to get some milk and a paper," said Lois. "It's about time you came down to collect your money."

"First they send an official to verify the ticket. Then they bring it to our house," said Daisy. "And it's a check. Tommy said they want pictures of us taking it in our living room."

Lois frowned. "I think it's boring to wait. And you should get real money, not a check."

"A check *is* real money," said Mr. Green, laughing. "The bank will take it just the same. And it will all add up the same in our account!"

"Here is the little lady who is responsible for the win!" Aunt Ivy was calling when she saw Lois.

Now everyone was talking to Lois and her family.

"We didn't know a thing about it till this very minute!" Lois's dad was saying.

A small band had set up in the frozen-food section and was tuning up. Soon they began to play, "We're in the Money," and couples began to dance down the narrow aisles. Tommy Tucker was handing out free soda pop, and Daisy noticed Delphie had a chocolate Fudgesicle in one hand and a peanut candy bar in the other. Aunt Ivy was trying to catch her nephew and get them away from him. "You are going to hyperventilate!" she called. "And have hyperglycemia!" She tried to hand him a bran bar instead, but he got away.

"All your teeth are going to fall out!" shouted Aunt Ivy. "And you'll get rickets!"

"I don't care!" said Delphie.

At last Mr. Green held up his hand and said, "I think we have to get home and go to bed now. This has been a very busy day!"

The crowd clapped and cheered and followed the Greens out the door.

Lois's parents drove them home. First they dropped Aunt Ivy off. Then they stopped at the Greens'.

"When you get the money, things will start happening," said Lois.

What did she mean, start happening? thought Daisy. More things were happening than had ever happened in Liberty before, and they didn't have a dime of the winnings yet!

CHAPTER 11

Daisy fell asleep as soon as her head hit the pillow. When she woke up in the morning the sun was streaming through her window and her parents and Delphie were already in the kitchen eating breakfast.

"Of course," her mother was saying, "a farm in the country would give me more room than the greenhouse on the roof."

"And I could have a studio out back—big enough to hold some pretty large animals," said Mr. Green.

"Larkspur could run all over the place," said Delphie. "He'd have a yard of his own, and we wouldn't have to take him for a walk on a leash."

Larkspur barked from under the table.

"You'd like that, wouldn't you, old boy?" said Delphie, patting him on the head.

Mr. Green picked up the real estate section of the paper.

"Hobby farm," he read. "Stable for three horses. Six acres. Brick home in A-l condition. Just turn the key and move in."

Daisy pictured her family in a new shiny car driving to the country. She pictured acres of corn and three horses and a big doghouse for Larkspur. There might even be a real barn, and a real cow!

But if this new life was going to be so wonderful, thought Daisy, why did she feel like she had a lump in her chest where her heart should be? Why did her stomach feel like it was full of knots?

"Hey!" yelled Delphie suddenly. "Here's the lottery man! And some people with cameras!"

This time there was no party. Just the photographers snapping pictures of the Greens in their condo.

"The more crowded the better," said one of them, trying hard to get all of the sculptures into one photo. "The public loves to see people win who are . . . ah . . . needy."

"We're not needy!" said Delphie.

"He means it looks like we could use a bigger house," said his father. "It looks like we can use the money."

Everyone trooped up to the roof garden and posed next to a giant beefsteak tomato plant growing in a wooden tub.

"And now for the big moment!" said the lottery man.

He handed Mr. and Mrs. Green the check, and the photographers snapped a shot of it going from the man's hand to Mrs. Green's.

A tax man had come with the lottery man and the photographers. At this point he spoke up and said, "I'll go to the bank with you."

"That's to be sure he gets his money first," said Delphie. "Lois told me."

At the bank there were more pictures and more handshaking and the check was put into the Greens' account. Then Mrs. Green wrote three checks.

One for the tax man.

One for Aunt Ivy.

And one for Lois.

"If it wasn't for Ivy and Lois, we would not be here today," she said. "I mean in the bank with all this money," she added.

Daisy looked at the checks.

The biggest one was for the tax man.

But the other two were for a lot of money, too. Aunt Ivy and Lois were rich along with the Greens!

"Don't forget the two dollars you owe Aunt Ivy!" piped up Delphie.

Everyone laughed and patted Delphie on the head.

"I think this check will cover that," said his dad.

On the way home, the Greens stopped at Lois's house to give her the money.

"Why, you shouldn't do that!" her parents cried as the photographer took their picture with tears in their eyes.

"Why do they take pictures when people are crying?" asked Delphie.

"People like emotion," said Lois.

"We'll put this into the bank for Lois for college," said Mr. Fable.

Lois was smart enough already, thought Daisy. What would she be if she went to college? There would be no living with her!

The next stop was Aunt Ivy's, and she burst into tears (right as the flashbulb popped) when she saw the check. "You only owed me two dollars!" she cried, hugging her sister.

"It's the least we could do," said her sister.

"You could buy a parking meter of your own!" said Delphie.

Daisy thought that was a silly suggestion, but everyone else laughed. People were ready to laugh at anything today, she thought.

When the Greens finally got home, and everyone else left, the phone began to ring.

"Invest your money with us!" said a woman's voice. "You won't be sorry."

The next call was from a man saying, "I am with Acme Real Estate Company and I have a piece of property that would suit you to a T!"

At first Mr. Green was patient and explained they had not decided what to do with the money yet. As more calls came in, he became less patient and took the phone off the hook.

Then Lois came to the door calling for Daisy.

"I saw just the house for you, on Dulcie Street," she said. "And it has a For Sale sign in the front yard!"

CHAPTER 12

"Can I come to look at the new house?" asked Delphie.

"Sure," said Lois. "Tell your mom we'll be back soon."

As they walked down the street, Lois tried to explain why the Greens should hurry up and buy a house.

"It's important to invest the money so it can grow," she said. "You can't just let it sit in the bank with low interest rates. Property is a hedge against inflation."

All this money talk was giving Daisy a headache. Houses, studios, greenhouses, inflation. Life seemed so simple last week. Now it was very confusing.

They came to Dulcie Street. It was the fanciest street in Liberty. Rich people lived there with police dogs and security systems.

"Here is the house for you!" said Lois, pointing. "It has a swimming pool in the yard."

"I don't like it," said Delphie. "It's pink. I don't want to live in a pink house."

Lois stamped her foot. "You can paint it! Just look how big it is and what a nice garden it has!"

Delphie shook his head. "It's got three garages. We don't need three garages. I can't drive. Neither can Daisy."

Lois sighed. "Someday you will have a car, Delphie, and you will wish you had listened to me and had this garage to put it in."

Daisy didn't say anything. She wondered if maybe she was getting the flu. Why else would she feel so queasy all over? It couldn't have anything to do with the lottery. Lottery winners always felt good. You could tell by their smiling faces in the paper and on TV.

When they got home, Aunt Ivy was there. She was saying to Mr. and Mrs. Green, "And that's my first purchase. I'm buying the best police radio on the market. This one will pick up signals from as far away as Hawaii!" She held up a catalog.

Daisy went through the living room to her own little bedroom. She threw herself on the bed and tried to figure out what was the matter.

She still didn't feel very good, and somehow Aunt Ivy's shopping talk just made her feel worse. So many thoughts were jumbled up in her head. Finally Daisy just closed her eyes.

Before long she fell asleep and began to dream. She dreamed that the lottery man came to their house. He dragged her dad's precious animals out of their condo and loaded them onto a truck to take to a big castle. It had lights shining out of the windows from crystal chandeliers, and glittering gold knives and forks instead of silver on the table. Her mother was there wearing lots of diamond necklaces, and there were five dishwashers lined up in the kitchen.

But Mrs. Green had a sad look on her face, and she kept trying to escape. Daisy and Delphie tried to help her to run back to her roof garden, but every time they got close the man would catch them and take them back.

When Daisy woke up she was worn out. But at least she knew what she felt. She didn't want a swimming pool in her backyard. She didn't want to move out of town to a farm! That would mean she would leave her school and Lois and her cozy little room! Her sweet family would not be gathered around the little table eating together!

Daisy walked out to the hall phone. It was quiet in the house. Everyone must be out looking at police radios with Aunt Ivy.

She dialed Lois's number and blurted out her problem.

"I don't want to move to the country!" she said. "And I don't want a swimming pool! I want to stay here."

Lois seemed to be thinking. Then she sighed.

"Do you know what's the matter with you?" she said.

No, she didn't, thought Daisy crossly. If she did, why would she be asking Lois?

"The matter with you," said Lois, "is that you worry too much."

What? That was it? Daisy stamped her foot. Lois didn't have any advice. She just had a complaint!

Daisy said good-bye and hung up the phone. She could hear static in the living room. It must be Aunt Ivy's new police radio. Her family was back.

Well, if Lois wouldn't help, she would have to take desperate measures. She would have to talk to her parents.

Daisy walked into the living room.

No one noticed her at first.

Delphie was wrestling with Larkspur.

Mr. Green was talking about the new metal cutter.

Mrs. Green was helping Aunt Ivy adjust the dials on her new radio.

"Just listen to that clear sound," Aunt Ivy was saying. "Why, if I was a detective I could be on the spot in minutes!"

Daisy cleared her throat.

Everyone looked up.

"Are you up from your nap, dear?" her mother asked. "You were sleeping so soundly we didn't wake you to go to town with us. Now, tell me which of these two samples you like best."

Her mother held up two paint chips. "For the walls in your room. I thought a pink stripe would be nice. With a floral bedspread and curtains."

"Wait!" Daisy burst out before she could stop herself. "I don't want pink stripes! I don't want to move! I want to stay in my same room here!"

Suddenly she had everyone's attention.

Her mother dropped the paint chips.

Her father forgot about metal cutters.

Aunt Ivy turned down her radio, and Delphie stopped wrestling.

They all stared at her.

"Everything is changing!" Daisy went on. She felt tears in back of her eyes just waiting to come out. She was glad the photographer was not around to watch for emotional outbursts. Daisy could have ended up on the front page of the paper!

Daisy's mother threw her arms around Daisy and hugged her.

"I think," she said slowly, "that we need to call a family conference. We all have to listen to Daisy and find out what is upsetting her."

"Fortunately we are all here together now," said Mr. Green. "Family meeting in the kitchen in five minutes!"

Daisy knew if her father called a family meeting, it must be a serious matter. The last family meeting was when the city was repaving and Delphie walked all over town in wet cement. The city had to do their sidewalk paving over again.

Aunt Ivy took out her notebook to record the meeting minutes. Her mother and dad poured cups of coffee for the adults and glasses of lemonade for Daisy and Delphie. Daisy didn't want lemonade. She wanted her room back.

Mr. Green pounded a potato masher on the table. "This meeting will come to order," he said.

Larkspur barked.

"Now, Daisy, tell us what is bothering you," said her mother.

"Nothing is going to be the same!" Daisy said. "I don't want a new house or a new life or new curtains."

"I can understand that," said her father, nodding.

"So can I," nodded Aunt Ivy.

"I want to move!" shouted Delphie. "Now we won't move just because Daisy doesn't want to!"

Daisy glared at her brother. This was her meeting, wasn't it?

Mr. Green pounded the potato masher again.

"We won't move anywhere unless we all agree," said Mrs. Green firmly. "And we don't have to do anything right away. We can leave the money in the bank and talk and plan and think and shop, but we don't have to do anything. No one can make us."

Daisy wiped her eyes. "Really?" she said.

"Really," said her mother. "This is a family decision."

"But what if we change?" Daisy asked.

"Is that what you're worried about, Daisy?" said Mr. Green. "That money will change us?"

Daisy nodded and sniffed.

"It won't," said Aunt Ivy, her arms around her radio.

"Well, I think it will," said Mrs. Green. "Daisy is right. Winning the lottery definitely changes a family."

"It will change our life," agreed Mr. Green. "But it does not have to turn us into different people. We have to hold on to what is important to us."

"That's right," said Mrs. Green.

"And anytime things move too fast," Mr. Green went on, "let's promise to talk about it. Talking clears the air. No sense in keeping things inside and worrying. Does everyone agree?"

Daisy nodded. So did Delphie.

"That makes sense," said Aunt Ivy. She looked anxious to turn more knobs on her radio.

Suddenly Daisy felt much, much better. Getting things off your chest did help. And her parents seemed to know as much as Lois. Maybe more!

She could look at houses on Dulcie Street and it did not have to change her life! And when the time came, they would be ready for the change. Her mother said so.

Aunt Ivy raised her hand. "I move that we bring this meeting to a close."

"I second the motion," said Delphie.

"It has been moved and seconded. Any objections?" asked Mr. Green.

Larkspur barked.

"That doesn't count," said Mr. Green. Everyone laughed.

And Daisy laughed hardest of all.

* * *

It was later in the afternoon, after Aunt Ivy left, that the phone rang. It was not an investment company. It was not Lois. It was Oriole Humphrey, the talk-show host from New York.

"You want us to come to New York to be on television?" said her mother. "All expenses paid?"

She hung up. "They want us all to be on the show," she said. "Lois and Aunt Ivy, too." Then she added, "We don't have to say yes, you know."

But Daisy knew they would say yes. A trip to New York? All expenses paid? The Statue of Liberty? A plane ride? What kind of fool would say no to that?

"I have to call Lois," she said.

"Wow!" said Lois when she heard the news. "That's the biggest talk show on TV! You know, I have this feeling our lives are going to be filled with adventure from now on."

Lois sounded like a fortune cookie! She might not know everything, but she was worth listening to. She had been right about the lottery win. Who knew what else she might be right about?

A shiver went down Daisy's spine.

A lottery win today, a television star tomorrow! And then what?

Would her father make gold alligators with diamonds for eyes?

Would her mother breed a new rose, called Fortune's Child?

Would Aunt Ivy be a private eye on her own TV series?

Only the fates knew. Well, and maybe God.

And Lois.